Tin Can Kids Book Club

FUN ON THE FARM ADVENTURES CHAPTER BOOK #1

Merry Mary

and the Strawberry Surprises

Story and Artwork by Denise Frances DiJoseph

This story is dedicated to all the farm families
who provide sustenance for their communities.
You are loved, respected, and appreciated.

To my happy husband, Phil, for making me laugh every morning
with his lightheartedness and for his unselfish generosity
to partake in countless hours of trout fishing that provided me
with the essential solitude to write this book.

A special thank you goes to English professor and author Richard J. Scholl,
for his vast knowledge and enthusiastic allegiance to the art of writing.

To my family and friends who cheered me on to write these
fun adventures for young readers to enjoy.

Merry Mary and the Strawberry Surprises
Written and Illustrated by Denise Frances DiJoseph

Published August 2025
Skippy Creek
Imprint of Jan-Carol Publishing, Inc.
All rights reserved
Copyright © 2025 by Denise Frances DiJoseph

ISBN: 978-1-962561-84-6
Library of Congress Control Number: 2025946789

Jan-Carol Publishing, Inc.
PO Box 701
Johnson City, TN 37604
publisher@jancarolpublishing.com
www.jancarolpublishing.com

CHAPTERS

1. The Chocolate Secret 1

2. Picnic at the Pond 7

3. The Sleepover 15

4. Betsy Finds the Chocolate 23

5. The Missing Strawberries 33

6. Betsy's in a Jam 41

7. Pickles, Paint, and Strawberry Pie 49

8. Let the Judging Begin! 59

9. The Strawberry Surprises 71

10. More Surprises 81

DEAR READER 88

FUN ON THE FARM PAGES 89

ABOUT THE AUTHOR 96

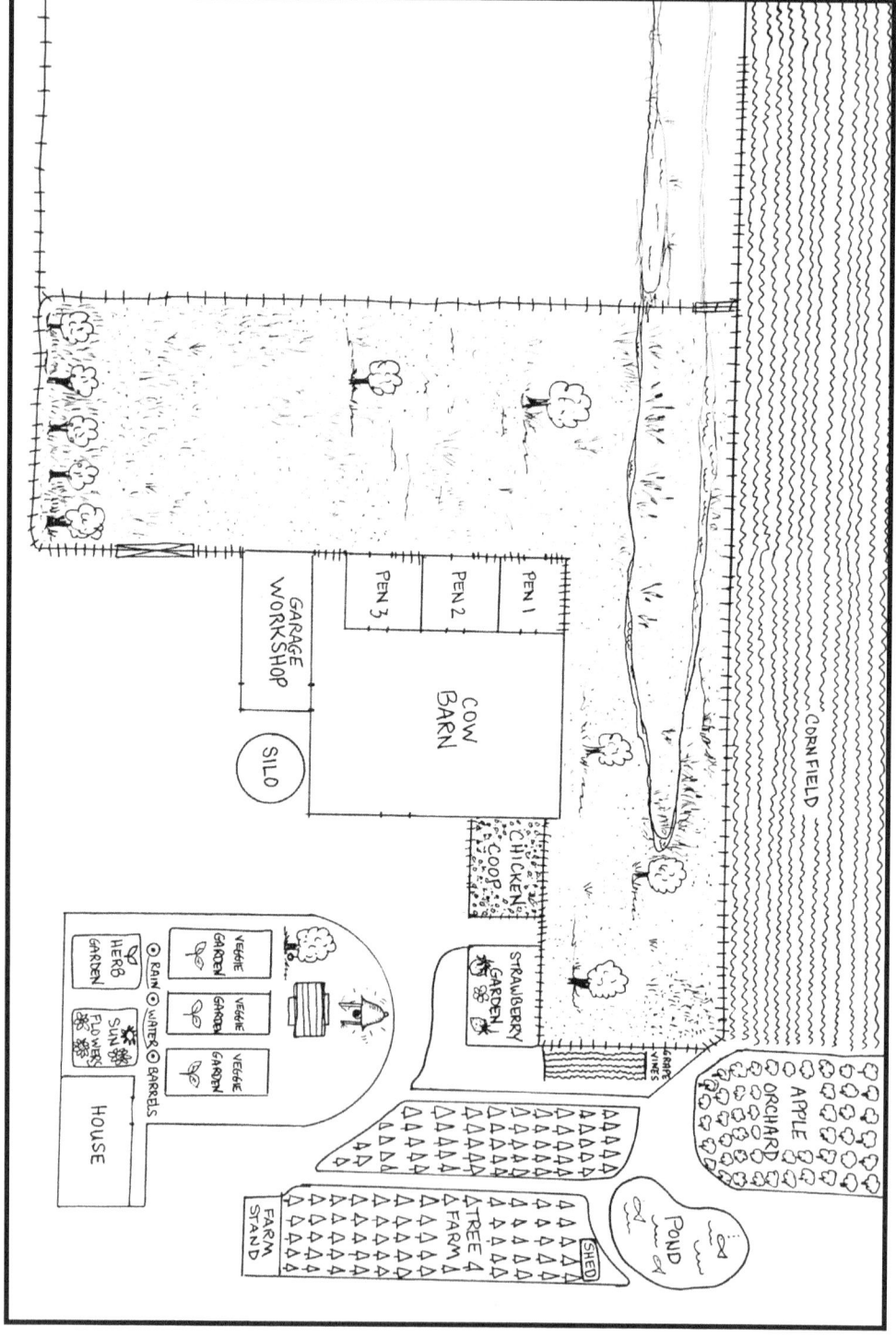

CHAPTER ONE
THE CHOCOLATE SECRET

"DING-DONG-DING-DONG-DING-DONG!" rang the doorbell.

Betsy looked out the window. "They're here!" she shouted to Maw. "Cody's carrying two picnic baskets—and I see backpacks, too!"

"Who's ready to pluck the cows and milk the chickens?" Uncle Phil asked as the front door swung open.

"That's very funny, Dad," laughed Katie-Lou.

"We're stacking the hay today," said Aunt Dee-Dee.

"The hay goes inside the corn crib, right?" asked Uncle Phil.

"No, silly, corn goes into the corn crib. You put hay inside the hay loft," said Betsy.

"That doesn't make any sense," said Uncle Phil.

"Before we get started…who wants a cold glass of chocolate milk?" asked Uncle Phil, looking inside the refrigerator.

"I do!" Betsy and Katie-Lou shouted at the same time.

"We'll meet you in the barn," said Maw. Aunt Dee-Dee and Cody followed her out the kitchen door.

"We'll be right there," said Uncle Phil.

The three sipped their milk. "Did you know that only brown cows give chocolate milk? I kid you not!" Uncle Phil said as he gulped the last drop. Then he stooped down and whispered, "Why do you think Paw feeds them chocolate candy? It's the best kept secret."

Betsy and Katie-Lou raised their eyebrows and stared at each other. "I never saw Paw give the cows any chocolate," stated Betsy. "And I never saw any cow give chocolate milk either."

"Of course you haven't!" he said. Uncle Phil put his hand up to his mouth. "It's an old farmer's secret from your grand-pappy," he winked. "C'mon, let's go to the corn loft!"

"Need any help, Mikey?" asked Cody.

"Nah, we're just about done," said Mikey.

The barn cats circled around and purred as Mikey poured leftover milk into their pan. Lottie, the family's black and white Border Collie, nudged her way into the crowd to drink some, too.

"Come here, Lottie," said Cody, kneeling down to pet her.

"Let's stack the hay before it gets too hot in the loft," said Paw.

"I'm tired already and we didn't even start!" laughed Uncle Phil.

It took all morning to stack the hay. The girls slid down the bales and threw pieces into the air, pretending it was party confetti. It was getting hot working up in the rafters. Maw and Aunt Dee-Dee left the barn to get lunch ready.

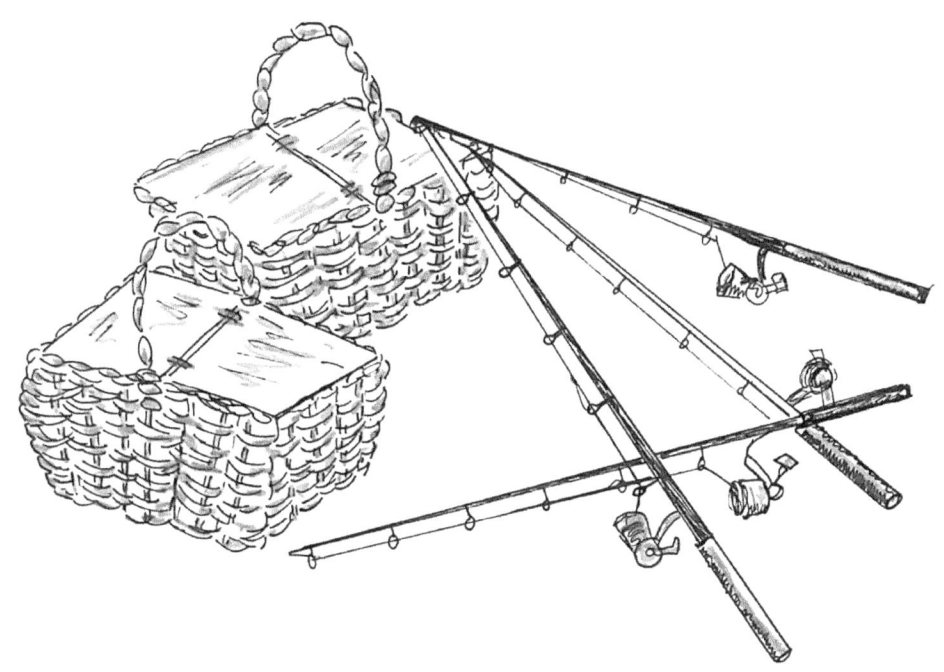

"That was a lot of work, but together, we got the job done," said Paw.

Everyone was sweaty and dirty from all the hay dust. Mikey blew his nose into his blue handkerchief. Katie-Lou sneezed. Lottie sneezed and rubbed her nose with her paw.

Maw and Aunt Dee-Dee brought out two tan picnic baskets and four fishing rods. "It's time to wash up! Let's have lunch by the pond today. You kids can fish for our supper!" said Aunt Dee-Dee.

Paw took off his orange hat and wiped his bald head. "I'm hungry!" he said.

"Me too!" said Uncle Phil.

"You're always hungry," laughed Cody.

CHAPTER TWO
PICNIC AT THE POND

Everyone stopped to look at Betsy's strawberry garden on the way to the pond.

"I think this is your best year ever. I see a lot more berries!" said Aunt Dee-Dee.

"How's the fence holding up?" asked Paw.

"So far, so good. Thank you for fixing it, Mikey," said Betsy.

"I don't think we'll be seeing any more rabbits in there. Mikey added extra wire where they dug a hole," said Maw.

"Mmmmm...strawberry rabbit pie," mumbled Uncle Phil, licking his lips. Uncle Phil was always joking, but sometimes he came up with good ideas.

"Ewwww! That's disgusting!" cried Katie-Lou.

"Actually, that might turn out to be a tasty stew," said Aunt Dee-Dee.

"We can make some for us to eat on a cold, snowy day. You'll have to freeze some extra strawberries for us, Betsy."

Everyone sat on the big picnic blanket and filled their plates with delicious food. Katie-Lou poured big cups of Sunny Honey Strawberry Lemonade for everyone. They ate chicken salad sandwiches, carrot sticks, and watermelon slices.

"Let's dig up some worms!" said Katie-Lou. Aunt Dee-Dee reached inside a picnic basket and gave the girls two empty tin cans to hold their worms.

"Here's some bait for you and Mikey," said Aunt Dee-Dee, handing Cody two tin cans filled to the top with chicken livers.

Cody was the best fisherman in the family. He somehow always knew where the fish were hiding and had the perfect cast, no matter which rod he used.

Cody and Mikey walked to the other side of the pond. A big maple tree fell into the water during last winter's ice storm. He knew that the underwater logs and branches were the perfect place for catfish to hang out.

Betsy and Katie-Lou caught a few bluegills. They threw them back because they were small.

Mikey reeled in a catfish. It was a good size, but not big enough to feed eight people.

Then it happened...

z-z-z-z-z-z-z-z-ZZZZZZZ!!!

Cody's rod almost bent in half. Something grabbed his bait. He reeled it in slowly while trying not to break the line.

There it was—a HUGE catfish! It was big enough to feed all eight of them with enough leftovers for Lottie, too.

"How much do you think it weighs?" shouted Paw.

"At least 10 pounds—maybe more," Cody yelled back.

Mikey looked at the size of his catfish. "That's another contest I didn't win," he mumbled while throwing it back into the pond. "I'll get you again when you're bigger," he said as it swam away.

"The winner of the fish contest for an extra dessert is… CODY!" shouted Katie-Lou, holding up his arm.

"Boo-hoo! I wanted to win," Uncle Phil rubbed his eyes, pretending to cry.

"Oh, Dad, stop. Here, I'll share my extra dessert with you." Cody threw a worm at his dad, who pretended to catch it in his mouth. Everyone laughed at their silliness.

"How is Merry Mary, Mikey?" asked Aunt Dee-Dee.

"She's doing great. I'm entering her in the farm show next week," replied Mikey.

"That's wonderful!" said Uncle Phil. "Maybe you'll win this year."

"She's a good cow," said Paw. "But the last time I talked to Sam's father, he said that Dottie was looking real strong." He looked at Mikey.

"We talked about this before. As much as you want to win—"

"I know," Mikey interrupted. "Don't be a sore loser if Sam and Dottie win again."

"That's right. There will be other shows if you don't place in this one," Maw said as she patted Mikey on the back.

"It's time to head out to the fields," said Paw, looking at his gold pocket watch. Everyone helped pack up the picnic baskets.

"Here's a big stick for your catfish, Cody," said Mikey.

Cody put the stick through the catfish. They lifted it up and carried it together on each of their shoulders for an easy walk back to the house.

"Don't forget to take your tin cans, kids," said Uncle Phil. "Hey, you know what? I'm calling you four The Tin Can Kids!" Everyone laughed.

"That's a great nickname!" said Maw. "They use tin cans all the time!"

Paw, Uncle Phil, and the boys drove the tractors into the fields. Maw and Aunt Dee-Dee stopped by the vegetable garden to pick green beans and tomatoes for supper.

Lottie, Betsy, and Katie-Lou ran to the chicken coop to give the hens some fresh water. They cuddled and petted each one until it was time for everyone to milk the cows again.

They all worked together to get the job done. Uncle Phil put two milker hoses on his head like horns and started mooing. Betsy rolled her eyes and laughed at how funny he looked. The girls grabbed their shovels and scraped the manure away from the stalls. Aunt Dee-Dee and Maw cleaned the teats. Mikey and Cody hooked up the hoses and switched them until each cow had her turn.

Uncle Phil squirted lotion dip on the teats when each cow was finished being milked. Paw gave them feed and clean water to eat and drink. Aunt Dee-Dee, Maw, Katie-Lou, and Betsy poured milk into the buckets and fed the calves. Mikey and Cody hosed everything down and sanitized the equipment.

Katie-Lou chased after the barn cats with Lottie. Betsy pretended to chase after the cats, but she was really searching for the chocolate candy that Uncle Phil talked about earlier.

"Hmmm, that's what I thought. There's no such thing as secret chocolate," Betsy announced to a cat that was curled up next to the empty milk pan.

"Let's go inside to help Maw make supper, girls," said Aunt Dee-Dee.

Betsy decided to keep looking for the secret chocolate later...

...when nobody was around.

CHAPTER THREE
THE SLEEPOVER

"That was a great supper!" yawned Paw.

Maw thanked Cody for the catfish. Uncle Phil thanked Cody for his half of the extra dessert.

"Time for The Tin Can Kids to shower and get ready for bed," said Maw.

Aunt Dee-Dee handed Cody and Katie-Lou their overnight backpacks as they headed upstairs.

An hour later, Betsy and her brother tiptoed out of their bedrooms and sat down at the top of the staircase. Cody and his sister sat with them.

If they were very quiet, they could hear their parents talking in the kitchen. Supper was over a long time ago, but their parents liked to sit there and nibble on leftovers.

15

"Mikey has a good chance to win this year," said Aunt Dee-Dee. Dishes and silverware clattered in the sink as Maw and Aunt Dee-Dee washed and dried them.

Maw said, "Sam's mom told me that he turns 12 in December, so this will be his last year competing in the Junior Division."

"If Mikey doesn't win, maybe he can win next year with Sam not being in the same age group," said Uncle Phil as he put his jacket on.

In the dim light coming from the kitchen, Betsy nudged her brother to get his attention.

"What do you think about that?" she asked him. He shrugged his shoulders and bit his bottom lip.

"Ah-ah-AHH-CHOOOO-oooo!"

Katie-Lou sneezed the loudest sneeze she ever sneezed, even though she tried to hold it back to not make any noise.

Cody laughed so much that he almost rolled down the steps. Lottie leaped from her favorite spot under the kitchen table and ran up the steps, barking at the four of them.

"Why are all of you still awake? Go to sleep!" said Maw.

"It's not a sleepover if you're not sleeping!" reminded Aunt Dee-Dee.

"I guess they don't want to go to Zinn's tomorrow," said Uncle Phil, getting out his car keys.

"Noooo! You know that's our favorite place!" Betsy shouted. They all jumped into their beds with a crashing thud.

"Goodnight, Tin Can Kids! Have fun tomorrow!" shouted Aunt Dee-Dee as she opened the front door.

"Save some donuts for me!" yelled Uncle Phil. "And don't bring home any more elephants or zebras from the auction!"

The Tin Can Kids heard the car tires make crunching sounds on the gravel driveway as Uncle Phil and Aunt Dee-Dee drove away.

Lottie paced back and forth in the hallway while Maw and Paw brushed their teeth and showered. When they turned off their bedroom light, Lottie plopped down in front of Betsy's door and let out a deep sigh.

It was dark…

…and silent…

…except for Betsy and Katie-Lou.

"Do you think Sam will win again?" Katie-Lou whispered.

"I hope not," replied Betsy.

Pond frogs croaked softly under the moonlight. They heard the gentle pitter-patter of rain tapping the windows.

Everyone was asleep…

…except for Betsy.

She stared at the shadows on the ceiling thinking about what she could do to help her brother win. Betsy closed her eyes and imagined him holding the Junior Champion banner, standing next to her holding her fifth blue ribbon prize for her strawberry jam. She soon drifted off to sleep smiling at the thought of everyone cheering for Mikey's first win.

Saturday morning, the six of them ate a quick breakfast.

"I know Sam is your best friend, Mikey, but I hope he DOES NOT win again!" Betsy said before slurping the last of her orange juice.

"Sam always wins…and he works hard to win," replied Cody after he swallowed his last bite.

Mikey didn't say anything. He quietly chewed his bacon, egg, and cheese sandwich.

"It's time to go. You know I don't like being late," said Paw. Lottie wagged her tail, looking at the last few crumbs of bacon on a plate. Betsy fed them to her as they were going out the door. They all piled into the car for the 30-minute drive to their favorite place.

"We're here!" shouted Katie-Lou. "I hope they have lots of animals at the auction."

"I hope we can find a parking space before the auction starts," said Paw.

"There's one!" Betsy pointed to a rusty truck backing out of a spot.

Mikey and Cody headed to their favorite food stand and bought a dozen gooey-fresh, soft donuts to share with everyone.

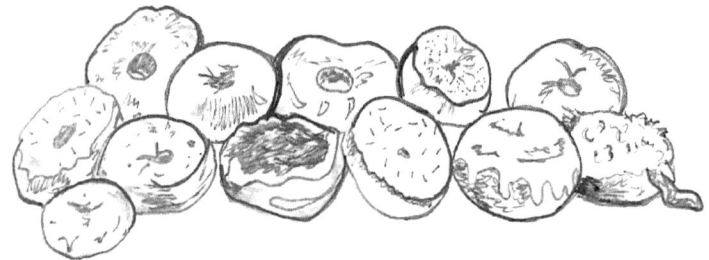

Paw walked over to talk to Sam and his dad, who were waiting for the auction to begin.

Katie-Lou poked her fingers inside the rabbit cages trying to feel their soft fur. Betsy looked for piglets but only found a bunch of ducks and a few noisy roosters.

"I wish I had some money to bid on a piglet," said Betsy to her mom.

"Why don't you think about setting up a table on Kid's Sell Day?" suggested Maw.

"Oooh, I'll help you earn some money for a baby pig!" said Katie-Lou. "We can sell carrots and sunflowers!"

"There's nothing for me at the auction today," said Betsy.

"Yeah, auctions are boring when you're not bidding on anything," said Katie-Lou.

"Let's go inside to shop at all the booths," said Maw. "We'll get lunch for everyone when we're done."

"We need soft pretzels and cotton candy, too!" said Katie-Lou.

At the auction, Sam bid on a box of sheep shearing tools and won. Paw bid on a bull gate and won. Mikey bid on a case of salt lick blocks, but someone else outbid him.

CHAPTER FOUR
BETSY FINDS THE CHOCOLATE

Betsy and Katie-Lou fell asleep on the drive home. Lottie greeted everyone in the driveway. She barked and circled around the car until everyone got out. Mikey and Cody headed toward the barn with Paw.

In the kitchen, Maw sliced a loaf of oatmeal bread that she and Aunt Dee-Dee made yesterday. The girls nibbled at some of the crumbs. "Why are you so quiet, Betsy?" asked Maw.

"We heard what you said last night. I don't want Sam to win again. I want Mikey to win. I feel sorry for him. I have four blue ribbons, and he has zero," Betsy explained.

"That's nice of you to want your brother to win, but it's best to let Mikey work on winning his own prize while you focus on your strawberries," Maw suggested.

"You do make the best-tasting strawberry jam, Betsy!" exclaimed Katie-Lou, licking her lips.

Maw spread butter on two slices of the soft bread and gave one to each of them.

"Can you teach me how to bake a strawberry pie?" asked Katie-Lou as she peeled off the crunchy crust and fed it to Lottie.

"Sure," said Betsy. "Only if you teach me how to paint a picture as good as you do!"

"That sounds like a fun plan to keep you both busy," said Maw. She went outside while the girls washed and dried the breakfast dishes.

Betsy stared out the window at her strawberry garden. Soap suds overflowed and ran down the side of the sink.

"Betsy!" shouted Katie-Lou as she quickly turned off the running water.

"Sorry, I was thinking about how happy I was when I won my first blue ribbon for my strawberry jam."

"Ohhhhhh, I get it—you want Mikey to know how it feels to win. Am I right?" asked Katie-Lou as she mopped up the sudsy water with a sponge.

Betsy nodded yes while still staring out the window. Katie-Lou put the last glass away and hung the dish towel to dry.

"Let's go check on the strawberries!" said Betsy.

The kitchen screen door slammed shut before Lottie could go out with them. "Sorry about that, Lottie," said Betsy as she opened the door for her.

Betsy slipped her feet into her favorite purple polka dot mud boots. Katie-Lou wore the extra pair of pink heart boots that were there just for her to use when she visited.

"Mikey doesn't say anything, but I know it bothers him that his friend wins every year," Betsy said.

Lottie wagged her fluffy tail and pushed her nose against Betsy's hand to be petted. "Mikey is just like you, Lottie. He takes good care of the animals. Merry Mary is the best cow he ever raised. He brushes her, gives her the best feed, and makes sure she's clean and happy. That's why he named her Merry, because she's a happy cow."

"And because she's always happy, she always gives the best milk out of the whole herd!" added Katie-Lou.

Lottie spun around in circles before running off barking toward the strawberry garden. Betsy and Katie-Lou tried to catch up, but Lottie was too fast. She was already waiting for them at the garden gate.

Betsy opened the gate and moved some of the drooping bird netting out of the way. Lottie pushed ahead of them and sniffed up and down the long rows of berries.

They saw a few white blossoms dotted here and there. Some of the berries were little and still green, but many were huge—bigger than the size of a hen's egg and turning bright red. They were almost ready to be picked to make a big batch of strawberry jam. Lottie finished inspecting the garden and plopped down by the gate.

"Looks like she didn't find any rabbits eating the berries this time," reported Betsy.

"Looks like we'll have a lot of juicy berries to pick soon," said Katie-Lou.

Betsy opened the gate, and Lottie ran off in a barking flash toward the barn where Paw was getting up on a tractor.

"What if my dad is right about brown cows giving chocolate milk?" said Katie-Lou.

"I never saw that happen on our farm," said Betsy.

"That's my point. You never saw it happen...

...but...

...if it's...

...a secret...

...maybe it's true?"

They stood at the gate and stared at the strawberries.

"If brown cows give chocolate milk…then maybe Red and White cows give strawberry milk," reasoned Katie-Lou.

"I don't know what to believe. I need to find the chocolate first," Betsy said. "C'mon, let's go look for it!"

Next to the barn door was a feed bag. Betsy opened the bag and sniffed. It smelled sweet, like pancake syrup mixed with grass, but it didn't smell anything like chocolate candy.

Katie-Lou saw Paw at the bullpen and ran over to him.

"Do you feed the cows chocolate candy?" she asked.

"When I can get some at the chocolate factory, I sure do," Paw answered.

"Where do you keep the candy?" asked Katie-Lou.

"I keep it in the cold storage room so it stays fresh," replied Paw. "Don't eat any. It's not chocolate for people."

Katie-Lou ran back to Betsy. "My dad is right! He wasn't kidding! It's TRUE! Paw said he feeds them CHOCOLATE!"

"I have to see it before I believe it," said Betsy.

Katie-Lou grabbed Betsy's hand. "C'mon, I'll show you where he keeps the candy!"

Betsy opened the big silver door. It felt so refreshing to step inside a cold room on such a hot day. There they were—10 feed bags with "J. DENGLER CANDY FACTORY: THIS CHOCOLATE IS NOT FOR HUMANS" printed on the sides.

Katie-Lou sniffed the bags. "It's chocolate alright—smell it." Betsy leaned over and sniffed. It definitely smelled like chocolate. "See? I told you my dad was right!"

Betsy's eyebrows went up. Her eyes got as big as the biggest strawberries she ever grew and smiled the biggest grin. She knew exactly how to help Mikey win, but that will be her own secret...

...Not even Katie-Lou will know her plan.

CHAPTER FIVE
THE MISSING STRAWBERRIES

After supper, they all piled into the car to take Cody and Katie-Lou home. Everyone talked about next week's farm show events. Maw read the long list of categories—best ice cream, fruits, vegetables, jams and jellies, baking, flowers, and lots of arts and crafts. Betsy looked out the window at the wildflowers waving in the wind along the road.

"Didn't you hear me, Betsy?" asked Maw. "You're entering your jam again this year, right?"

"Maybe…probably…yes…I guess I will," answered Betsy.

"You don't seem very excited about it," said Paw.

"Oh, I am. I was just thinking about something else," replied Betsy.

The next morning, Betsy woke up early to get started on her plan to help Mikey win. But she had to wait until after she helped milk the cows, feed the chickens, collect eggs, and care for the other animals. Then she dressed quickly for Sunday service and waited outside for everyone to finish getting ready.

Betsy was finally alone to pick a handful of berries. She walked over to Merry Mary who was grazing on grass. "Here you go, girl," said Betsy, letting her eat them out of her hand. Merry Mary gobbled them up. She LOVED them!

"Mooooooo!"

"Oh, does that mean you want more?"

Betsy ran back to the garden and picked another handful. Merry Mary ate them in one lick of her tongue.

"These berries will help you win at the farm show," Betsy said as she rubbed Merry Mary's ears. "Mikey is sure to win when you surprise the judges by giving them yummy strawberry milk!"

"Moooooooo!" replied Merry Mary, licking Betsy's hand for more.

"Let's go, Betsy!" shouted Paw as he jumped into the car.

"What were you doing with my cow?" asked Mikey.

"I was petting her," said Betsy. That wasn't a lie. She DID pet her, but she didn't mention giving her some strawberries.

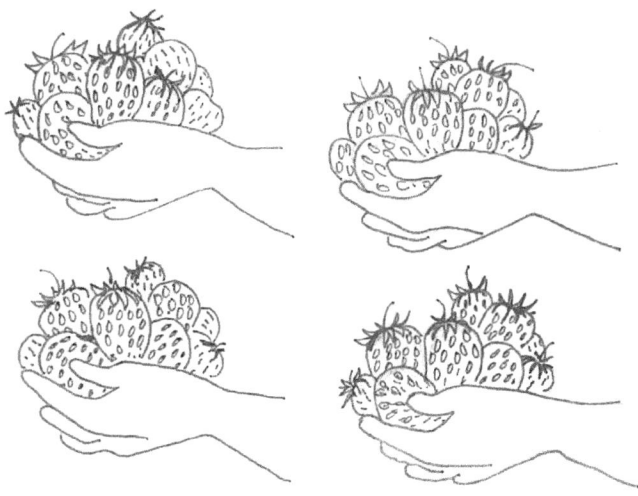

The next morning, Betsy checked on Merry Mary in the barn.

"How's her milk this morning?" Betsy asked Mikey.

"It's good—same as always," he replied.

Betsy checked on her strawberries. She picked four handfuls of berries and put them in a big tin can and carried them over to Merry Mary. "Here are some more berries for you!" Merry Mary gobbled them up faster than she did yesterday.

The next morning, she asked Mikey again about Merry Mary's milk.

"It's the same as it was yesterday, Betsy. Why do you keep you asking me?"

"No reason," said Betsy.

Mikey put his hands on his hips, scrunched his eyebrows, and shook his head, trying to figure out why she kept asking about his cow.

Something wasn't right. Betsy's plan wasn't working. She looked for Paw and found him in the workshop changing the oil on a tractor.

"Paw…I was wondering…how much chocolate do you feed to the Guernseys?"

"Oh, I don't know. It depends on how much I can get at the factory…maybe a scoopful for each cow."

Betsy walked back to Merry Mary. "I gave you more than a scoopful," she said, patting Merry Mary's belly.

"Moooooooo!"

"Hmmm…I guess that means you didn't get enough. Okay, girl, I'll get you some more."

So, Betsy picked another big tin can, full of dark red berries. She fed them to her before going inside the house to see if Maw needed any help.

"Today would be a good day for you to make your strawberry jam," said Maw. "Let's take a look at the garden."

Betsy did NOT want to do that. She knew there were no red berries left after picking all of them for Merry Mary to eat.

Maw opened the gate and cried, "OH NO! Something ate all your ripe berries! Hurry—go get Mikey in the barn." Betsy ran into the barn. Together they ran back to the garden. Mikey looked carefully at the fence.

"Everything looks good. I don't see any holes," he said while walking back to the barn.

Maw checked the bird netting. "There are no holes in the netting either. I don't understand why all the berries are gone."

Betsy knew exactly why there were no ripe berries to pick.
They were inside Merry Mary's belly.

"It looks like you'll have to make the jam tomorrow when these other berries are ripe. I was going to run some errands and buy lemons for you today, but there's no rush for me to get them now. I'll get them tomorrow," said Maw.

"Okay, thank you, Maw," said Betsy. But what Betsy really wanted to do was feed more berries to Merry Mary and not make any jam.

That night, Betsy stared at her bedroom ceiling. She tried to figure out how many berries she needed for the jam. And for Katie-Lou's pie. And for Aunt Dee-Dee's rabbit stew. And enough left over for Merry Mary to eat. She soon fell asleep having more questions than answers.

CHAPTER SIX
BETSY'S IN A JAM

"The farm show is coming up in a few days, Betsy. You really need to work on your jam today," said Maw as they cleared the breakfast table. "Paw and Mikey have a full day out in the fields, and I'm going into town to get your lemons. Why don't you pick the berries and then pull some weeds in the vegetable garden while I'm gone? When I get back, we can start making the jam."

Betsy watched Maw drive down the road. Lottie wagged her tail, begging for some table scraps. "I don't know what to do, Lottie!" Betsy sighed while feeding her pieces of leftover scrambled eggs. "Let's go to the garden to see how many berries we have to work with today."

Lottie looked up at her and burped. She must have known that Betsy was worried about something because, instead of racing to the garden, she walked quietly at Betsy's side.

Betsy counted the red berries. Lottie sniffed up and down the rows looking for rabbits. "I don't think I have enough strawberries to make 24 jars of jam like I usually do."

"Let's see…That's 12 jars for Uncle Phil and Aunt Dee-Dee, and 12 jars for us. That's one jar for each month for a whole year. If I put some aside for Katie-Lou's pie and Aunt Dee-Dee's stew, there won't be any berries left to give to Merry Mary before the farm show!"

Lottie trotted over to Betsy and rubbed her nose against Betsy's cheek. "Ugh, what am I going to do, Lottie?" she cried. Tears ran down her cheeks. "I want to make jam for everyone, but I also want to help Mikey win." She cried even louder. Lottie licked her tears away. Betsy stopped crying and looked up.

"What are you saying, Lottie? Do you know a way for me to make everyone happy?" she sniffled.

"Woof-Woof-Woof-Woof-Woof!"
"Woof-Woof-Woof-Woof-Woof!"

Lottie barked 10 times. "Are you saying I should make 10 jars of jam instead of 24?" Lottie lowered her body and laid her head on the ground. "So you're saying I should make 10 small jars?" Lottie wagged her tail and yipped.

"Hmmm. Let me figure this out. If I make 10 small jars of jam, save some for Katie-Lou's pie, and some for Aunt Dee-Dee's stew…that means…I WILL HAVE ENOUGH FOR MERRY MARY TO WIN WITH HER STRAWBERRY SURPRISE! Yes, that's what I'll do! Thank you, Lottie!"

Betsy picked the berries for the jam. She picked the berries promised to Katie-Lou and Aunt Dee-Dee. The rest of the berries were not quite ripe, but they would soon be ready to pick for Merry Mary to eat. She put the bucket of berries in the kitchen sink. Then she pulled weeds in the vegetable garden until Maw came home.

Lottie barked at Maw, who was pulling into the driveway. Betsy carried the groceries inside. Maw looked at the berries in the sink.

"There's not much to work with this year, is there, Betsy?"

"Some of them are for Katie-Lou and Aunt Dee-Dee. I think maybe I can make 10 small jars."

"Ten is better than none," said Maw.

Betsy got out Granny-Maw's recipe card and made the jam while Maw worked on baking some rosemary olive oil bread.

GRANNY-MA'S STRAWBERRY JAM
1 CUP of LOVE
1 POUND of STRAWBERRIES
1 POUND of SUGAR (ADJUST TO YOUR LIKING)
1 SQUEEZE OF HALF A LEMON

WASH + DRAIN BERRIES. REMOVE GREEN TOPS.
SMASH BERRIES IN A SAUCEPAN. BRING TO A
SLOW BOIL AFTER ADDING SUGAR + LEMON. DO
NOT BURN! POUR INTO STERILIZED JELLY JARS.

After supper, Betsy wanted to check on Merry Mary before it got dark, but a rumbling thunderstorm forced her to stay inside.

She watched flashes of lightning in the dark gray sky and listened to the rain hit against her bedroom window. She worried that Merry Mary's strawberries might turn into a mushy mess from all the rain.

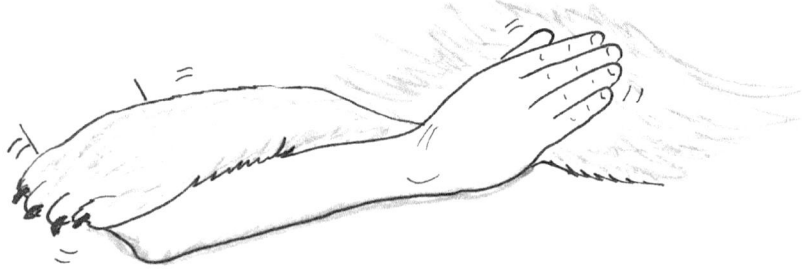

Lottie jumped up on the bed. "All this effort to help Mikey win, and the last of the berries might be ruined," she told Lottie while petting her. Lottie put her paw on Betsy's arm. "You're right, Lottie. I should think about good thoughts."

The next morning, Betsy woke up with good thoughts. All day long, she imagined Merry Mary surprising the judges with her strawberry milk. She pulled weeds in the garden and then fed her more strawberries. She imagined Mikey holding his first place Junior Champion banner and fed her even more strawberries. She washed the supper dishes and imagined standing next to him holding a blue ribbon for her strawberry jam. That night, Betsy stared at her bedroom ceiling and soon fell asleep smiling about all these good thoughts.

CHAPTER SEVEN
PICKLES, PAINT, AND STRAWBERRY PIE

"Why are all these pickle jars on the kitchen table, Maw?" asked Betsy.

"DING-DONG-DING-DONG-DING-DONG!" rang the doorbell. It was Uncle Phil, Aunt Dee-Dee, Cody, and Katie-Lou.

"Why are you here today holding four backpacks?" asked Betsy.

"Surprise! We're having a big sleepover tonight!" shouted Katie-Lou.

"We're here to help around the farm, and tomorrow, we'll all go to the farm show together!" said Aunt Dee-Dee.

"That's just great," said Betsy.

"Whoa, you don't seem happy that we're here," said Uncle Phil, looking sad.

"No, of course I'm happy. It's great that you're all here," she explained with a deep sigh.

But Betsy was not happy about having more people around. She didn't want anybody to see her feeding berries to Merry Mary—not even Katie-Lou. She wanted it to be a strawberry milk surprise for everyone.

All afternoon, Aunt Dee-Dee and Maw picked cucumbers to make lots of dill pickles and sweet relish. Uncle Phil and Cody joined Paw and Mikey out in the cornfield.

It was the perfect time for Betsy to teach Katie-Lou how to make their Granny-Maw's strawberry pie. They had fun slicing the berries, squeezing the lemons, adding sugar, and rolling out the dough to make the crust. Katie-Lou put the pie inside the oven and set the timer.

Maw and Aunt Dee-Dee piled a mountain of cucumbers into the sink. "Mmmm...That strawberry pie smells delicious!" said Aunt Dee-Dee. She hugged Betsy. "Thank you for showing her how to bake Granny-Maw's pie."

"I brought all my art supplies with me, Betsy. What do you want to paint?" asked Katie-Lou.

All Betsy could think about was feeding Merry Mary more strawberries. "I don't know...maybe paint my strawberry garden?" Betsy replied.

"That's a great idea!" said Katie-Lou.

"You get everything set up at the picnic table while I go check on something," said Betsy.

Katie-Lou opened her art box. She put the paints, brushes, a pencil, a paper towel, and a canvas board next to two jars filled with water.

Betsy ran to her garden to secretly pick some strawberries. She was happy to see that last night's rain did not ruin the berries. They were a beautiful shade of dark red bursting with juice. She put them inside a tin can and hid it under her shirt.

51

"What are you doing, Betsy?" asked Katie-Lou. Betsy jumped and turned around.

"Don't sneak up on me like that!" Betsy yelled.

"Sorry, I didn't mean to scare you. I thought you were waiting for me." She handed Betsy a pencil and a canvas board.

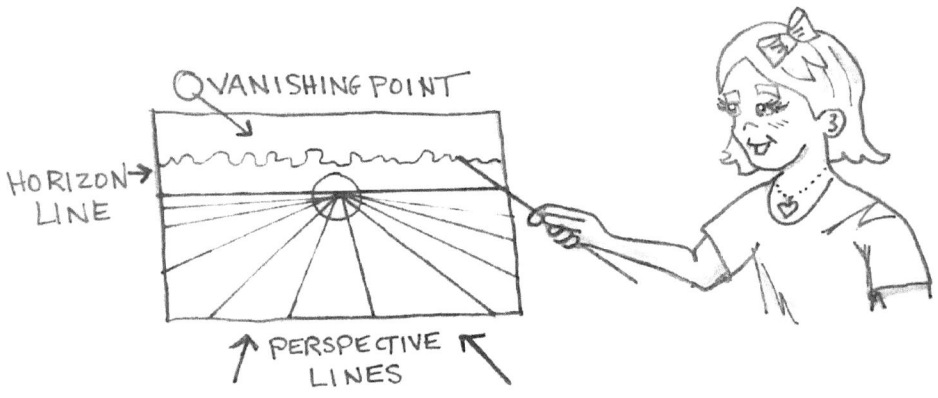

Katie-Lou closed one eye looking at the field and ran her finger across the air tracing the tree line. "Do you see where the treetops touch the sky? That's called a horizon line."

Betsy drew a crooked line across the board. "Duh, that was easy," she said, rolling her eyes just a little.

Katie-Lou showed her how to make the garden look long by drawing the front wider than the back. "It's called perspective," Katie-Lou explained. "It's how you can make something look close up and far away."

Betsy scrunched up her nose. "I'm not sure where to begin."

"Let's start with the garden gate," suggested Katie-Lou. "That's the closest thing to us. Draw it bigger than the tiny tree line you just did." Betsy drew long rectangles close together to make a big gate.

Katie-Lou pointed to the eight long rows of strawberry plants. "Do you see where all the lines get closer together? That's called a vanishing point."

"There's more to painting a picture than I thought," sighed Betsy.

"It's just like following a recipe," said Katie-Lou. "You have to follow each step until it's done—just like baking a pie."

The tin can under Betsy's shirt was getting hot. All she could think about was feeding Merry Mary more strawberries. "Now that my drawing lesson is over, why don't you wait for me at the picnic table and get the paints ready? I'll be there in a minute," Betsy said.

Katie-Lou walked back to the picnic table with Betsy's canvas board. Before she could sit down, she heard a loud BUZZZZZZZZZ that made her jump up. The oven timer buzzed loudly like a bunch of honey bees. It was time to take the pie out of the oven.

Aunt Dee-Dee helped Katie-Lou lift the heavy pie onto the counter. Katie-Lou turned off the stove and helped herself to another slice of buttered bread to eat at the picnic table while she waited for Betsy.

She watched Betsy run over to Merry Mary who was waiting at the meadow fence and mooing.

"Here you go, girl. There's not much today, but I promise you'll get all the berries tomorrow morning." Betsy wiped her hands on her shirt while walking past the vegetable garden.

"Why are you spending so much time with Merry Mary?" asked Maw, holding another basket of cucumbers.

"I tell her every day that she's going to win first place at the farm show," replied Betsy.

"I'm sure she likes all the attention you're giving her. Look at her. She's still mooing for you!" laughed Aunt Dee-Dee.

Betsy knew exactly why Merry Mary was still mooing.
She wanted more strawberries.

Katie-Lou dipped the paintbrush into the red paint. Then she added white paint. Betsy mixed it together.

"See? It made pink!" said Katie-Lou. "I'll show you how to make any color you want." Betsy painted with shades of green for the plants, light blue for the sky, bright red for the berries, and white for the flowers. "It looks great! You did a good job, Betsy!"

"It's beautiful!" said Maw. "Thank you for teaching Betsy."

"Let's put it in a safe place so it can dry overnight," said Aunt Dee-Dee.

After supper, Maw opened one of the jars to check on Betsy's jam. It was still a little goopy. "Sometimes it needs an extra day for it to gel," said Aunt Dee-Dee.

"It should be better tomorrow," said Katie-Lou.

"I hope so," said Betsy.

It was a long day. Everyone was tired. The parents were so tired that they did not stay up late snacking on leftovers and talking in the kitchen. Everyone was in bed by 8:30 p.m.

Aunt Dee-Dee and Uncle Phil slept on the pullout bed on the screened-in porch. That was their favorite sleepover place. She liked watching the deer graze in the fields under the moonlight. Uncle Phil snored sometimes, and when he did, he blamed the noise on the pond frogs.

Betsy paced in her bedroom.

"What's wrong?" asked Katie-Lou.

"I can't sleep. I keep thinking about Mikey and Merry Mary. I really want them to win tomorrow."

"Is that why you fed her a berry treat?"

"How do you know I fed her strawberries?"

"I saw you feeding them to her today. You had a tin can of them hidden under your shirt the whole time you were drawing your picture."

"Oh, Katie-Lou, I can't hide this from you anymore. I fed her strawberries all week long, and she is still not giving any strawberry milk," Betsy confessed.

"Oh, so you're the critter eating all the berries!" giggled Katie-Lou. "I heard Maw tell my mom that something's been eating all the berries, but you're the one making them disappear! Now it makes sense that you only had enough berries to make 10 jars of jam!"

"Shhhh! I want this to be a strawberry milk surprise for everyone," whispered Betsy.

"Don't worry, Betsy. I know your plan will work. A cow has four stomachs, you know. It might take a while for the strawberries to work their way through."

"That's not true. A cow doesn't really have four stomachs, but there are four parts of the stomach," Betsy said, correcting her.

"Well, then...It still takes time for food to go through all four parts," Katie-Lou said. "I'll help you feed the last of the berries to her tomorrow morning when nobody is watching, okay?"

"Okay, thanks. You're the best, Katie-Lou. And thank you for teaching me how to paint today."

"Thank you for teaching me how to bake a strawberry pie! I can't wait to share it with everyone after the farm show tomorrow."

"Goodnight, Katie-Lou."
"Goodnight, Betsy."

Betsy let out a deep sigh. She did everything she could to get Merry Mary ready to surprise the judges with her strawberry milk.

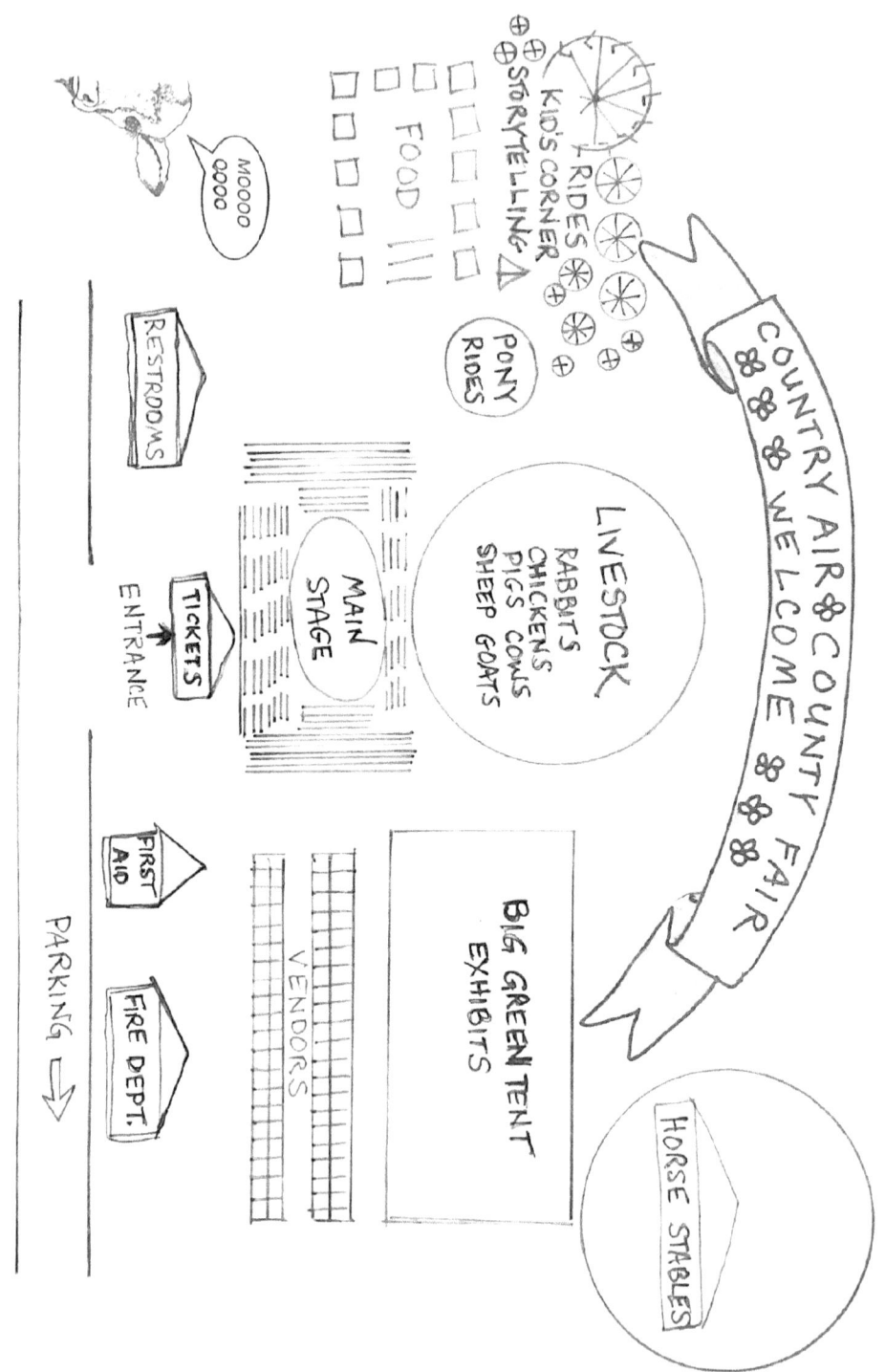

CHAPTER EIGHT
LET THE JUDGING BEGIN!

"Good morning, it's time to wake up, my little busy bees!" said Uncle Phil. "Let's get this farm show on the road!"

After breakfast, Betsy and Katie-Lou picked the last of the berries. "I had a silly dream last night that the whole field turned into strawberry milk. Even the fence turned pink!" said Betsy.

"Everything will be okay. Go put these berries in the car, and I'll go check on Merry Mary for signs of strawberry milk. I'll be right back," Katie-Lou said to Betsy.

Betsy paced back and forth waiting for good news.

"Well…anything?" Betsy asked.

"Not yet," sighed Katie-Lou.

Betsy let out a deep sigh and looked down at the ground.

Paw, Uncle Phil, Mikey, and Cody piled into the truck after getting Merry Mary into the trailer. "She seems a bit fussy," said Mikey.

"I hope she's not getting sick," said Paw.

Aunt Dee-Dee, Maw, Betsy, and Katie-Lou followed them in the car. Maw's rosemary olive bread and Betsy's jam and berry basket were in the trunk along with Aunt Dee-Dee's quilt, Cody's duck decoy carving, and Katie-Lou's sunflower painting.

It seemed like the ride took forever. Maw and Aunt Dee-Dee droned on about starting a new project—something about setting up hives for honey bees. Katie-Lou fell asleep halfway there. Betsy stared out the window. All she cared about was feeding Merry Mary the last of the strawberries.

"Wake up, Katie-Lou! We're finally here!" shouted Betsy as they drove under the big entrance sign.

COUNTRY AIR COUNTY FAIR

Paw and Mikey led Merry Mary to the cow area. Cody and Uncle Phil headed toward the horse stables. They wanted to talk to the handlers because Cody wants to be a farrier when he's older.

Betsy and Katie-Lou fed the basket of fresh berries quickly to Merry Mary while Paw and Mikey signed papers at the check-in table.

"I'm sure the strawberry milk surprise will happen the moment the judges are standing in front of her. This is so exciting! Mikey is sure to win!" said Katie-Lou.

Paw and Mikey walked back to be with Merry Mary.

"Did you notice if Sam signed in yet?" asked Mikey.

"I don't see him anywhere," Paw replied as he looked all around the fairgrounds.

"Merry Mary is still acting strange. Do you think it's a stomachache?" asked Mikey.

"I'm not sure. Just keep an eye on her," said Paw.

Betsy grabbed onto Katie-Lou's arm. They ran to a big shade tree. "OH NO! What have I done?" cried Betsy. "I'm making Merry Mary sick from eating all the strawberries I've been giving her! I feel terrible!" Betsy paced back and forth. "This was a bad idea—all because I want Mikey to win. Poor Merry Mary...This is awful!"

Katie-Lou rubbed Betsy's back. "You were just trying to help. But...it's too late now. You can't change what's been done. Let's hope for the best. Maybe she's restless from all the excitement around her. It's not her quiet meadow at home, you know."

"You're right. Maybe she doesn't like all the noise here," Betsy said with a weak smile. She looked up and saw Maw waving to them to come over. "Let's go be with our moms under the big green tent."

"I can't find your berry basket, Betsy," said Maw. "You wanted me to enter them in the fresh fruit category, right?"

"Uh, no...We took care of the berries," said Katie-Lou.

That wasn't a lie, but saying it that way made Maw and Aunt Dee-Dee think she meant that they had eaten them.

"You sure did take care of them. Look at your hands," said Aunt Dee-Dee.

Betsy and Katie-Lou looked at their hands and giggled. Their fingers were stained bright red from feeding the juicy berries to Merry Mary.

"Paw said that Sam and Dottie didn't sign in yet," said Betsy.

"Hmmm...Sam is never late for anything," said Maw.

"We're going back to be with Paw and Mikey to watch the judges," said Katie-Lou.

"Okay, but come back to be with us as soon as you can," said Aunt Dee-Dee.

The girls returned just in time for the judges to begin. Paw and Mikey were busy talking to some friends. Betsy walked over to one of judges and tapped on his clipboard.

"Excuse me, sir. I want you to know that cow #143 gives delicious strawberry milk."

"Oh, really?" the judge chuckled. His moustache wiggled when he laughed.

He called the other judges over. "Come over here. You have to hear this!" he said to the group.

They circled around Betsy and leaned in close to hear her better.

"Now, tell us why #143 gives delicious strawberry milk."

Betsy looked up at all the judges staring down at her.

Katie-Lou nudged her. "Go on—tell them—now's your chance!"

"Well, you see…Our Guernseys are all brown, and Paw feeds them chocolate candy to make chocolate milk. And #143 eats strawberries to make strawberry milk. You see, when you mix red and white paint together, you get pink, right? So, a Red and White Holstein gives pink strawberry milk!"

The judges stood up and looked at each other.

"BWAH-HA-HA-HA-HA-HA-HA-HA-HA-HA!"

They laughed so loudly that all the cows in line started mooing and the crowd stopped talking to look at them.

"Oh, that's a good one!" said one of the judges.

The tall judge said, "I'm sorry to say, but feeding strawberries to a cow will not make strawberry milk."

Another judge added, "And brown cows do not give chocolate milk, either."

"Thanks for making us laugh, but we have many cows to look at," said another judge as they headed toward the first cow in line.

Paw and Mikey walked over to the girls. "What are you doing talking to the judges? You can't do that! I'll get disqualified!" yelled Mikey.

"No worries, Mikey. It was just a misunderstanding," said one of the judges, still laughing.

"What did you say to the judges, Betsy?" asked Paw.

Betsy looked down and rubbed her toe into the dirt. She didn't want to tell him.

Uncle Phil and Cody returned from the stables.

"What's going on?" asked Uncle Phil.

"Betsy was just about to tell us what she said to the judges about Merry Mary."

"Oooh...Talking to the judges is a big no-no," said Cody, shaking his head.

Just as Betsy was about to tell them what she said, it was Mikey and Merry Mary's turn. The judges asked Mikey many questions and wrote important notes on their score cards.

They asked him what he fed her and how he brushed her to keep a shiny coat. The judges looked at her weight, the length of her leg bones, the shape of her head, neck, chest, feet, and udder. They even talked about how beautiful her healthy eyes sparkled and shined in the sunlight.

"That's just great, Katie-Lou," said Betsy. "All this time, I thought I was doing something good, and I did NOTHING to help Mikey win—NOTHING! I was selfish—just SELFISH! All I have to show for it is 10 small jars of jam to share with my family. I should have asked Paw about chocolate milk cows before I wasted all those strawberries. I made a BIG mistake!"

"But I DID ask Paw, and he said he feeds them chocolate," Katie-Lou pleaded.

"Feeding chocolate to cows is not the same as cows giving chocolate milk," sighed Betsy.

"You're right. We wanted it to be true so much that we weren't thinking about what was truly true and what was not."

"The only good thing is that Sam isn't here. Mikey still has a chance to win first place!" Betsy said, smiling.

All they could do was to wait and hope for the best.

The judges finished talking to Mikey. Paw asked Betsy again what she said to the judges. She confessed everything. She told them how the secret chocolate milk cows gave her the idea to feed Merry Mary lots of strawberries to make strawberry milk in time for the judging. Katie-Lou told them that Betsy did it because she wanted Mikey to win.

Paw looked at Uncle Phil.

Mikey looked at Cody.

They all looked at Betsy and Katie-Lou.

"BWAH-HA-HA-HA-HA-HA-HA-HA-HA-HA!"

They burst out laughing so loudly that all the cows in line flicked their tails and the judges stopped judging to see who was making all that noise.

"No wonder the judges laughed!" said Paw.

"I was just trying to help Mikey win," said Betsy.

"Well, if I win, it will be because I have the best cow in the show today—without any strawberry milk surprises for the judges!" Mikey said proudly while scratching Merry Mary's ears to comfort her.

CHAPTER NINE
THE STRAWBERRY SURPRISES

"WE ARE ANNOUNCING THE WINNERS OF THE BIG GREEN TENT DIVISIONS IN FIVE MINUTES," a booming voice said over the loudspeaker.

Betsy and Katie-Lou ran back to Maw and Aunt Dee-Dee.

"Where have you been?" asked Maw. "They're ready to announce the winners!" Paw, Uncle Phil, and the boys joined them just in time.

"FIRST PLACE IN THE BREAD CATEGORY

OF THE BAKING DIVISION IS…

FRANCES BERKS!"

"That's my mom! Maw, you won first place!" shouted Betsy.

**"FIRST PLACE IN THE YOUTH PIE CATEGORY
OF THE BAKING DIVISION IS...KATIE-LOU WINFIELD!"**

"WHAAAAT!!!??? I didn't enter any pie. It must be a mistake. How did I win?" asked Katie-Lou.

"Surprise! I entered your pie in the contest," said Maw.

**"FIRST PLACE IN HANDMADE QUILTS
OF THE ARTS AND CRAFTS DIVISION IS...
DEE-DEE WINFIELD!"**

"YAY! You won first place, Aunt Dee-Dee!" shouted Betsy.

**"FIRST PLACE IN THE JUNIOR DUCK DECOY
WOODCARVING CATEGORY IS...
CODY WINFIELD!"**

"Good job, Cody!" shouted Uncle Phil.

**"FIRST PLACE IN THE YOUTH PAINTING CATEGORY
OF THE ARTS AND CRAFTS DIVISION IS...
KATIE-LOU WINFIELD FOR HER SUNNY SUNFLOWERS!"**

"Congratulations, Katie-Lou!" shouted Paw. "I always liked that one."

"SECOND PLACE IN THE YOUTH PAINTING CATEGORY

OF THE ARTS AND CRAFTS DIVISION IS…

BETSY BERKS FOR HER STRAWBERRY GARDEN!"

"WHAAAAT!!!??? I didn't enter my painting. It must be a mistake. How did I win?" asked Betsy.

"Surprise! I entered your painting in the contest," said Aunt Dee-Dee.

"There sure are a lot of strawberry surprises today," laughed Paw, clapping his hands.

It seemed like it took forever for the loud voice to announce all the winners in the other categories.

"Let's go back to Merry Mary," said Mikey.

"Wait…What about Betsy's jam?" asked Cody.

"WE HAVE ONE MORE CATEGORY. FIRST PLACE IN

THE YOUTH JAMS AND JELLIES IS…

ELLA HOUCK!"

"WHAAAAT!!!??? That can't be right!" said Katie-Lou.

"SECOND PLACE IN THE YOUTH JAMS AND JELLIES IS…

ANNA YODER!"

"Huh?" Betsy said as her jaw dropped open. Katie-Lou's jaw dropped too.

**"THIRD PLACE IN THE YOUTH JAMS AND JELLIES IS…
OLIVER JAMES!"**

Betsy dropped her shoulders and lowered her head. "My jam didn't win anything," she mumbled.

"It's a good batch. I think it just needed more time to gel," said Maw.

**"HONORABLE MENTION IN THE YOUTH JAMS AND JELLIES IS…
BETSY BERKS!"**

"Well now, that's a different kind of a strawberry surprise," said Paw as he lifted his hat and scratched his head.

**"WE WILL ANNOUNCE THE WINNERS IN THE JUNIOR DIVISION
IN THE LAMB AND COW CATEGORIES IN FIVE MINUTES."**

Everyone hurried back to be with Merry Mary. Mikey was steps ahead of everyone. He didn't like being away from her for such a long time.

Merry Mary was happy to see everyone. She mooed softly and twitched her ears to keep the flies away from her face.

"FIRST PLACE FOR JUNIOR MEAT LAMB DIVISION IS…
SAM PENN!"

"Ahhh, so THAT'S where Sam has been this whole time!" shouted Mikey.

"No wonder we didn't see Dottie," added Uncle Phil.

"FIRST PLACE FOR THE JUNIOR RED AND WHITE COW
DIVISION IS…MIKEY BERKS!"

Mikey almost fell over.

He couldn't believe it.

He finally won!

"CONGRATULATIONS, Mikey, you did it!" Cody shouted.

"Mikey's the man!" said Sam as he walked up to the group. He shook Mikey's hand.

"Good job," said Sam's dad.

"We're proud of you," said Sam's mom.

Maw hugged Sam's mom. Then she hugged Mikey. Aunt Dee-Dee hugged Mikey. Uncle Phil patted him on the back. Betsy and Katie-Lou jumped up and down, holding his hands. It was a merry moment for Mikey when they handed him the prize banner.

"Why didn't you enter Dottie for a sure win, Sam?" asked Mikey.

"Oh, I wanted to work with the lambs this time," replied Sam. Sam's mom winked at Maw. Betsy and Katie-Lou saw that.

"What do you think that wink was all about?" whispered Katie-Lou.

"Hmmm...maybe somebody else wanted Mikey to win too," whispered Betsy.

A man wearing a bright yellow shirt and hat walked up to Mikey and Sam. "Hello, my name is Joe Harvey. I'm a reporter for the Sunny Day News. I'd like to interview both of you for a feature article in our Sunday paper."

"C'mon, Tin Can Kids!" shouted Uncle Phil. "Let's go back to the tent to take some pictures while we wait for Mikey."

"I'll stay here with Sam's parents while our boys talk to Mr. Harvey. We'll catch up with you in a few minutes," said Paw.

"Let's get Betsy and Katie-Lou together first with their artwork," said Uncle Phil. The girls held up their paintings with their prize ribbons waving in the breeze.

"Take a picture with their strawberry pie and jam too," said Aunt Dee-Dee.

"What about Maw and Mom?" asked Katie-Lou.

Maw and Aunt Dee-Dee held their prized bread and quilt while Uncle Phil took a picture.

"It's Cody's turn," said Katie-Lou.

Cody held up his duck decoy carving. "C'mon, give us a smile," said Uncle Phil. Cody gave a bashful half-smile.

"It's okay to be happy about doing a job well done," said Aunt Dee-Dee.

Katie-Lou made funny faces at her brother until he gave a big smile.

"Great picture!" said Maw.

"Let's go back to Merry Mary and Mikey to get a few pictures of all the winners together!" shouted Uncle Phil.

They watched Mr. Harvey shake Mikey's hand.

"How did the interview go?" Maw asked Mikey.

"Mr. Harvey asked a lot of questions. I felt like I was talking to another judge," he laughed.

Mikey stood beside Merry Mary holding his first-place banner. Cody stood on the other side of her with his duck decoy carving. Betsy held her garden painting and jam jar. Katie-Lou propped the sunflower painting against her leg and held her strawberry pie with two hands.

"Hurry, Uncle Phil," shouted Betsy. "The pie is heavy, and Katie-Lou might drop it!"

"We don't want that to happen. Okay, everybody…Say CHEDDAR CHEEEEESE!" shouted Uncle Phil.

CHAPTER TEN
MORE SURPRISES

Lottie barked and spun around in a circle to greet everyone as they pulled into the driveway.

Mikey walked Merry Mary to her stall. "Thanks for a great day. You did a good job!" he said, rubbing her ears.

Everyone was tired, but there was one more job to do before supper. The cows had to be milked.

Uncle Phil put a milker hose on his forehead to look like a unicorn and started singing, "When the mooooon hits your eye like a strawberry pie, that's a-moooo-zing." Betsy laughed at how funny he always changed the words to one of his favorite songs.

They all worked together to get the job done. The girls grabbed their shovels and scraped the manure away from the stalls. Aunt Dee-Dee and Maw cleaned the teats. Mikey and Cody hooked up the hoses and switched them until each cow had her turn.

Uncle Phil squirted lotion dip on the teats when each cow was finished being milked. Paw gave them feed and clean water to eat and drink. Katie-Lou and Betsy poured milk into the buckets and fed the calves. Mikey and Cody hosed everything down and sanitized the equipment. Maw and Aunt Dee-Dee went inside to get supper ready.

Everyone sat around the kitchen table while Lottie hid underneath in her favorite spot. They ate a big garden salad, spaghetti and meatballs, and Maw's rosemary olive oil bread with homemade garlic butter. For dessert, they ate Katie-Lou's strawberry pie—or what was left of it after the judges had some.

"The judges shared one piece, so now there's only enough for seven slices, and there are eight of us," said Katie-Lou.

"It's okay. Sniff-sniff," whimpered Uncle Phil. "I'll give up my slice as my time-out for causing all this strawberry milk trouble."

"You're giving up your dessert? Well, that's another strawberry surprise," laughed Paw.

"No, I'll give up my slice," said Betsy. "I should have asked if brown cows give chocolate milk before I did anything."

Uncle Phil perked up. "Did you say that I can have your slice, Betsy?"

"I think she did," laughed Aunt Dee-Dee.

"I have an idea," said Cody. "Why don't we make smaller slices so everyone can have dessert?"

"That's a great idea!" said Maw as she cut into the pie. Lottie gobbled up some pie crust as soon as it hit the floor.

"Here we thought the rabbits ate the berries, and it was Betsy and her strawberry milk surprise plan all along," said Maw.

"I'm sorry that I fed Merry Mary all the strawberries instead of making jam for everyone. I didn't think that through. I was selfish," said Betsy.

"You were trying to help me win, and I understand that you did that out of kindness," said Mikey.

"That blue ribbon pie was delicious, Katie-Lou!" said Uncle Phil as he licked his plate clean.

"I'm sorry that I was joking too much. I really thought you knew I was kidding when you rolled your eyes and said that you never saw cows give chocolate milk," he said to Betsy.

"We can't believe everything that we hear," added Cody.

"That's true," said Katie-Lou. "We wanted it to be true, but we didn't have real proof."

"Well, Mikey and Merry Mary proved that they were winners today," said Aunt Dee-Dee.

"Let's celebrate!" said Katie-Lou.

"Let's celebrate with a cold glass of...strawwwwwberry milk!" said Uncle Phil.

Katie-Lou poured eight glasses from the milk pitcher.

"Congratulations to Mikey!" said Cody.

"Cheers to our family!" said Betsy.

Everyone looked at Paw to take the lead in the Moo-Moo Game. "Who's going to be the last cow singing this time? Are you ready?" he asked.

They took a deep breath.

"Together…on the count of three…

…one…two…three!

MMMMMMMMOOOOOOOOOOOOOOOOOOOOOooooo!"

Everyone shouted their longest moo. Katie-Lou was the first one to stop, followed by Aunt Dee-Dee, then Maw, Betsy, Uncle Phil, Paw, then Cody, then Mikey. Lottie was still howling. She was the last cow singing this time!

They all laughed and laughed and laughed.

And that is the end of the story about Merry Mary and the Strawberry Surprises.

...Until the phone rang.

Maw answered the phone. "It's Sam. He wants to talk to Betsy."

Betsy looked puzzled.

"Talk to him," coaxed Cody.

Betsy slowly picked up the phone.

"Hello? Yes…Uh-huh…Thank you…I'm glad you won, too… Okay…Oh wow, really?…I'll ask…Thank you, Sam…Bye!"

"What did he say?" asked Mikey.

"Porkchop had a litter while we were all at the farm show. He wants to know if I want one of her piglets to raise so that I can enter her in the Fall Festival Farm Show."

Betsy looked at Maw and Paw. "Can I please have a baby pig?" begged Betsy.

"We'll talk about it tomorrow at breakfast," said Paw.

"On that note, I think it's time we call it a great day," said Uncle Phil, yawning and stretching as he stood up.

Everyone walked out to the car. Aunt Dee-Dee hugged Betsy. "You are a kind sister for wanting to help your brother win. Here, I want you to have this." Aunt Dee-Dee reached inside the trunk and handed her the prize-winning quilt.

"But, Aunt Dee-Dee…I thought you wanted to sell it at the quilt shop in town?"

"I can always make another one. This one is for you."

"Thank you, Aunt Dee-Dee! I promise to take good care of it!"

That night, Betsy hung her two new ribbons next to the four old ribbons and climbed into bed. She looked at all six ribbons swinging in the breeze from the ceiling fan—four old first-place ribbons, one new second-place ribbon, and one new honorable mention ribbon. Lottie wagged her tail and put her head under Betsy's hand to be petted.

"These ribbons will remind me to make better decisions and try new things too," she whispered to Lottie.

Betsy listened to the pond frogs croak softly under the full moon. She thought about names for Porkchop's piglet and soon fell asleep under her new strawberry quilt

* * *

Dear Reader,

I was bored with everything. I couldn't go outside to play for a long time, so I thought it would be fun to paint pictures of farm animals. I started by painting a meadow with a cow eating green grass.

But there was a problem. The cow asked to be in a pink meadow eating a strawberry! No matter how hard I tried to paint it the way I wanted it to look, the green meadow and her mouth didn't look right. I painted the grass pink and put a strawberry in her mouth, and guess what happened? It looked really good! The cow looked so happy! And I was happy to try new things!

Another word for happy is "merry," and "merry" sounds like the name Mary, so I named her Merry Mary. Every day when I sat at my art easel to paint her picture, Merry Mary would tell me more about her story living on a farm.

I hope that you have as much fun writing and drawing your story adventures as I did creating this book to share with you. Maybe someday I will get to read your story. That would be awesome!

Your Writer Friend,

Denise

FUN ON THE FARM

MAW AND AUNT DEE-DEE'S
RECIPE BOX

Sunny Honey Strawberry Lemonade

About 10 Lemons
About 20 Strawberries
About ¼ - ½ Cup Honey
Water
One Gallon Pitcher
Mesh Strainer
Fork
Long Wooden Spoon or Spatula
One bowl to hold about 20 strawberries

SAFETY IN THE KITCHEN!

ALWAYS HAVE A RESPONSIBLE
ADULT HELP YOU MAKE THIS FOOD

Always wash your hands with soap and water
before working in the kitchen.

1. Rinse and peel lemons
2. Put a mesh strainer over the pitcher
3. Use your hands or a fork to squeeze and mash the lemons over the strainer.
   This catches the seeds and pulp.
4. Put strainer aside
5. Rinse strawberries
6. Pull off the green tops and put the berries into a bowl
7. Use your hands or a fork to mash the berries until there are no lumps
8. Put the mashed berries into the pitcher
9. Add honey to the pitcher
10. Add water to fill the pitcher halfway
11. Stir with a wooden spoon or spatula
12. Fill the pitcher with water

FUN ON THE FARM

HOW TO MAKE A STRAWBERRY BOOKMARK
BY BETSY

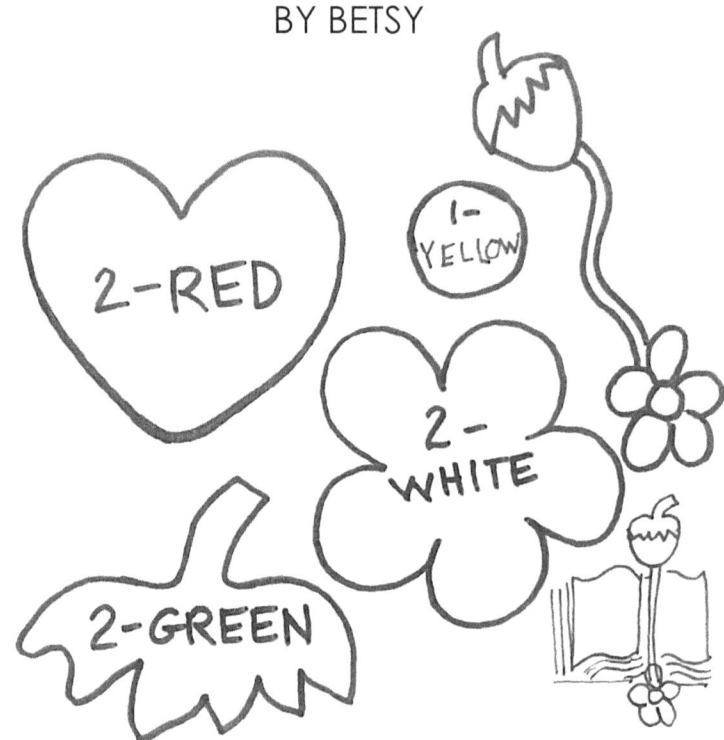

FELT: ONE OF EACH COLOR (RED, WHITE, GREEN, YELLOW)
WHITE GLUE * SCISSORS * PENCIL

- TRACE THE SHAPES ONTO THE FELT AND CUT OUT THE PIECES
  (CUT THE GREEN RECTANGLE PIECE A LITTLE LONGER TO FIT THE LENGTH OF YOUR BOOK)

- GLUE ONE HEART ON TOP OF THE LONG GREEN RECTANGLE

- GLUE THE OTHER HEART ON THE BACK OF THE FIRST HEART

- GLUE THE GREEN BERRY TOPS ON TOP OF EACH HEART PIECE

- GLUE ONE FLOWER PIECE TO THE OTHER END OF THE RECTANGLE

- GLUE THE OTHER FLOWER PIECE ON THE BACK OF THE FIRST FLOWER

- GLUE THE YELLOW DOT IN THE CENTER OF THE FLOWER ON ONE SIDE

* SAFETY REMINDER *
ALWAYS KEEP YOUR ART SUPPLIES SAFELY AWAY FROM LITTLE KIDS AND ANIMALS
TO AVOID INJURY, SWALLOWING, OR CHOKING ON THEM

FUN ON THE FARM

HOW TO MAKE A TIN CAN COW PENCIL CUP
BY KATIE-LOU

ONE CLEAN TIN CAN (SAVE THE LID FOR A FUTURE PROJECT)

WHITE GLUE

FOAM BRUSH

SCISSORS

ONE PIECE OF BROWN OR BLACK FELT

ONE PIECE OF WHITE FELT

MARKER OR PENCIL

SMOOTH LID CAN OPENER TO REMOVE THE LID
(USING A CAN OPENER THAT MAKES SMOOTH LID TOPS HELPS TO AVOID SHAR

STEP ONE:
- ROLL THE CAN OVER THE WHITE FELT TO MEASURE & CUT WHAT YOU NEED TO COVER THE CAN
- CUT A STRIP OF THE LEFTOVER WHITE FELT LONG ENOUGH TO GO AROUND THE INSIDE TOP
- HAVE A RESPONSIBLE ADULT HELP YOU WITH THE NEXT STEP!
- PUT SOME GLUE AROUND THE INSIDE TOP EDGE OF THE CAN USING THE FOAM BRUSH
- GENTLY PLACE THE FELT PIECE OVER THE GLUE
- LET IT DRY WHILE YOU WORK ON THE NEXT STEP

STEP TWO:
- SMEAR THE OUTSIDE OF THE CAN WITH A THIN LAYER OF WHITE GLUE USING THE FOAM BRUSH
- USING CLEAN HANDS, ROLL THE CAN OVER THE RECTANGLE PIECE OF MEASURED WHITE FELT
- LET IT DRY WHILE YOU WORK ON THE NEXT STEP

STEP THREE:
- CUT OUT BLOB SHAPES FROM THE BLACK OR BROWN FELT TO MAKE THE COW PRINT PIECES
- PUT GLUE ON THE BACK OF THE COW PRINTS AND STICK THEM ALL OVER THE WHITE FELT CAN
- LET IT DRY OVERNIGHT

YOU CAN FILL THE CAN WITH FLOWERS, PENCILS, OR YOUR FAVORITE ROCK COLLECTION!

* SAFETY REMINDER *
ALWAYS KEEP YOUR ART SUPPLIES SAFELY AWAY FROM LITTLE KIDS AND ANIMALS
TO AVOID INJURY, SWALLOWING, OR CHOKING ON THEM

FUN ON THE FARM

LET'S MAKE A FUN FISHING GAME
BY CODY AND MIKEY

FIND A LONG STICK THAT YOU'D LIKE TO USE FOR YOUR FISHING POLE
ONE BALL OF JUTE OR COTTON CRAFT STORE STRING
PAPERCLIPS (JUMBO SIZE OR USE WHATEVER YOU HAVE)
PLASTIC WATER BOTTLES WITH CAPS: USE DIFFERENT SIZES IF YOU WANT
WHITE GLUE
DIFFERENT COLORS OF TISSUE PAPER & FOAM CRAFT BRUSH
MOD PODGE GLOSS SEALER & FOAM BRUSH (OPTIONAL)

- TIE A LONG PIECE OF STRING TO ONE END OF THE STICK
- TIE A PAPER CLIP TO THE END OF THE STRING AND BEND IT TO FORM A CURVED LETTER J HOOK
- TIE A PIECE OF STRING AROUND THE MOUTH OF EACH BOTTLE TO MAKE A LOOP
- PUT THE LIDS BACK ON TO HOLD THE LOOPS IN PLACE
- GLUE TISSUE PAPER PIECES ALL OVER THE BOTTLES
- ADD FINS AND TAILS BY FORMING THEM OUT OF BLOBS OF TISSUE PAPER AND GLUE
- LET THE FISH DRY OVERNIGHT. YOU GET TO FLATTEN THEM THE NEXT DAY!
- FLATTEN THE BOTTLES WITH YOUR HANDS OR FEET TO MAKE THE FISH BODIES
- PUT A COAT OF MOD PODGE SEALER OVER THE DRIED PAINT IF YOU WANT TO MAKE THEM SHINY
- LET THE FISH DRY OVERNIGHT AGAIN

TO PLAY THE GAME:
- PUT ALL THE FISH IN A BIG PILE OR IN A SMALL PLASTIC BABY POOL.
- TRY TO HOOK AS MANY FISH AS YOU CAN UNTIL THEY'RE ALL GONE OR TIME IS UP.
- YOU CAN PUT NUMBERS ON THE FISH TO SEE WHO HAS THE MOST POINTS.
- THINK ABOUT OTHER WAYS TO PLAY THE FISHING GAME.

* SAFETY REMINDER *
ALWAYS KEEP YOUR ART SUPPLIES SAFELY AWAY FROM LITTLE KIDS AND ANIMALS
TO AVOID INJURY, SWALLOWING, OR CHOKING ON THEM

FUN ON THE FARM

HELP LOTTIE HERD THE COWS
BY PAW

FUN ON THE FARM

A COLORFUL MEMORY GAME
BY UNCLE PHIL

RED (3)	BRIGHT RED (3)	DARK RED (2)
1. PAGE 38 STRAWBERRIES 2. 3.	1. 2. 3.	1. 2.
RED & WHITE (4) 1. 2. 3. 4.	**ORANGE (2)** 1. 2.	**PINK (4)** 1. 2. 3. 4.
DARK GRAY (1) 1.	**LIGHT BLUE (1)** 1.	**BLACK & WHITE (1)** 1.
PURPLE (1) 1.	**YELLOW (1)** 1.	**SILVER (1)** 1.
GOLD (1) 1.	**BLUE (3)** 1. 2. 3.	**WHITE (3)** 1. 2. 3.
GREEN (5) 1. 2. 3. 4. 5	**BROWN (6)** 1. 2. 3. 4. 5. 6.	**TAN (1)** 1.

WHAT PAGE CAN YOU FIND THE NAME OF A COLOR?
AND WHAT OBJECT IS THAT COLOR?

HINT: THERE ARE THREE PAGES THAT MENTION THE COLOR RED.
ONE ANSWER IS: PAGE 38, STRAWBERRIES.

THE TIN CAN KIDS BOOK CLUB SERIES

BOOK #1: *MERRY MARY AND THE STRAWBERRY SURPRISES*

BOOK #2: *PEARL THE SHOW PIG*

BOOK #3: *THE HOLIDAY DEER SAFETY FOR BELLA & BUTTONS*

BOOK #4: *HEETHORN & HAWTHORN GUARD THE HEN HOUSE*

BOOK #5: *EIGHTY THOUSAND FRIENDS*

BOOK #6: *HARE'S HAIR EVERYWHERE! THE TROUBLE WITH RABBITS*

BOOK #7: *GOOD MORNING, GOOD NIGHT, GOOD GRIEF! RAY THE ROOSTER*

BOOK #8: *THE FARMER'S MARKET MIXUP*

BOOK #9: *THE APPLE-ATCHA ORCHARD HOOFER THE DANCING HORSE*

BOOK #10: *SHOWTIME AT THE FAMILY REUNION*

DID YOU DRAW A PICTURE ABOUT MERRY MARY AND THE STRAWBERRY SURPRISES?

SHARE YOUR ARTWORK ONLINE WITH OTHER READERS!

SEND YOUR PICTURE TO:*
TinCanKidsBookClub.com

* SUBMISSIONS & POSTINGS WITH PARENT/GUARDIAN VERIFIED APPROVAL ONLY.
FIRST NAME AND LAST NAME INITIAL WILL BE POSTED.
SOCIAL MEDIA TAGGING IS SOLELY AT THE OPTION OF THE ADULT SUBMITTER.

@tincankidsbookclub
TinCanKidsBookClub.com

ABOUT THE AUTHOR

Denise Frances DiJoseph is an artist and author residing in East Tennessee. She was born and raised in Chester County, Pennsylvania, where her talent for art and writing sprouted the moment her kindergarten teacher read *Harold and the Purple Crayon* by Crockett Johnson.

She merited Summa Honors with a BFA in Studio Arts and a minor in Art History. Numerous professors encouraged her to include her flair for writing in her pursuits. Denise earned a coursework certificate from The Children's Institute of Literature soon after university graduation. The lessons introduced her to the intricacies of writing for children and sparked the joy of illustrating and storytelling. She is a member of Lost State Writer's Guild and SCBWI (Society of Children's Book Writers and Illustrators).

Her favorite subject was, and still is, "Show and Tell." This was an early muse that led her to implementing and facilitating grant-funded art programs for at-risk women and girls and presenting as a keynote speaker at universities and conferences. It also gave her the courage to dress up as a silly restaurant entertainer creating colorful balloon animals on "Kids Eat for Free Days."

Her favorite vegetable is birthday cake. Her favorite color is all of them because she can't decide which one she likes best.

Denise retired from owning an art school and gallery before dipping her ink pen into writing and illustrating stories for children. A lifetime of vast interests and experiences springboards her creative expression. She enjoys learning new things and is forever grateful to be able to share her kaleidoscope of adventures with young readers.